Merry Meet Again

POEMS FOR SMALL CHILDREN TO RECITE

Selected and Arranged by

Elizabeth Hough Sechrist

with Illustrations by

Guy Fry

" Merry have we met, and merry have we been,
Merry let us part, and merry meet again;
With our merry sing-song, happy, gay and free,
And a merry ding-dong, happy let us be! "

Granger Index Reprint Series

Originally published by

MACRAE-SMITH-COMPANY
Philadelphia

BOOKS FOR LIBRARIES PRESS
FREEPORT, NEW YORK

INTERNATIONAL STANDARD BOOK NUMBER:
0-8369-6272-9

LIBRARY OF CONGRESS CATALOG CARD NUMBER:
77-160908

PRINTED IN THE UNITED STATES OF AMERICA

To
JOANNE HOUGH CRANCH
and
LINDA HOUGH HAMMATT

HAPPY SONGS

Piping down the valleys wild,
Piping songs of pleasant glee,
On a cloud I saw a child,
And he laughing said to me:

" Pipe a song about a Lamb! "
So I piped with merry cheer.
" Piper, pipe that song again; "
So I piped: he wept to hear.

" Drop thy pipe, thy happy pipe,
Sing thy songs of happy cheer."
So I sang the same again
While he wept with joy to hear.

" Piper, sit thee down and write
In a book that all may read."
So he vanish'd from my sight,
And I pluck'd a hollow reed,

And I made a rural pen,
And I stain'd the water clear,
And I wrote my happy songs
Every child may joy to hear.
—*William Blake*

PREFACE

IF we were to put into one book all the poems we love, what a big book that would be! In *Merry Meet Again* we had space for only a very few of the Mother Goose rhymes, but I am sure a great many, such as " Jack-be-Nimble," and " Mary, Mary, Quite Contrary," are written in your memory. If you are Still Very Young and like rhymes and jingles, the poems in the first part of our book will be your favorites.

If you go to school you will want to learn some of the poems selected for School Programs. Among these you will probably find just the right ones for entertainments, too. And if you are going to make a speech, I hope there will be one to suit you in the Speech section of the book.

Boys and girls are often asked to recite on some special day like Christmas, Mother's Day, Children's Day or Rally Day. Seventy of the poems here are for red-letter days.

[vii]

At the end of the book you will find Prayers and Table Blessings. I am sure you already know at least one prayer. Perhaps among these you will discover one that you will want to have for your very, very own.

I think the easiest way to learn a poem is to read it over and over again until it is singing a little song in your head; a song that you never, never forget. If you like the poems in this book you will want to read them many times, and before you realize it you will know them " by heart."

For a merry time, then, with *Merry Meet Again!*

ELIZABETH HOUGH SECHRIST.

August, 1941.

ACKNOWLEDGMENTS

THE editor wishes to express her appreciation to the following publishers and authors for their kind permission to include poems bearing their copyright: The Bobbs-Merrill Company, for "It" from BOOK OF JOYOUS CHILDREN by James Whitcomb Riley, copyright 1902, 1930; used by special permission of the publishers; Follett Publishing Company, Chicago, for "Meeting the Easter Bunny" from AROUND THE TOADSTOOL TABLE by Rowena Bastian Bennett; Henry Holt and Company, Inc., for "Some One" from A CHILD'S DAY by Walter de la Mare; Houghton Mifflin Company, for "Thanksgiving" by Ralph Waldo Emerson; J. B. Lippincott Company, for "Lincoln's Birthday" by John Kendrick Bangs; Lothrop, Lee & Shepard Company, for "Farm Voices" from THE RUNAWAY DONKEY by Emilie Poulsson; The Macmillan Company, for "Night" from STARS TONIGHT by Sara Teasdale; "Fourth of July" from RHYMES ABOUT OURSELVES by Marchette Gaylord Chute; "The Little Turtle" from COLLECTED POEMS (1925) by Vachel Lindsay; "I'd Laugh Today," "Mix a Pancake," "My Gift," "The City Mouse," and "The Stars" from SING SONG by Christina G. Rossetti, by special permission of the publishers; Macrae-Smith-Company, for "Foolish Flowers" from ALL 'ROUND OUR HOUSE by Rupert Sargent Holland; Oglethorpe University Press and Miss Anne Robinson, for "April and May" from LITTLE MISS APRIL by Anne Robinson; Frederick A. Stokes Company, for "Earth and Sky," reprinted by permission from COME CHRISTMAS, by Eleanor Farjeon, copyright, 1927, by Frederick A. Stokes Company; The American Boy Magazine, for "Some Things That Easter Brings" by Elsie Parrish reprinted from The Youth's Companion; The Churchman Magazine, New York, for "Thangsgiving Time"; The Curtis Publishing Company and Mrs. Rowena Bennett, for "Harvest Prayer" by Rowena Bennett reprinted from the magazine Jack and Jill; The Unity School of Christianity, for "Every Day" by Elizabeth Haas, "Table Blessing" by Julia Budd Shafer, "Table Blessing" by Bernice Ussery and "We Thank Thee" by Carmen Malone, reprinted from the magazine Wee Wisdom; Mr. Gelett Burgess for his kind permission to include "I'd Rather Have Fingers Than Toes," "My Feet," and "The Purple Cow" reprinted from his NONSENSE RHYMES; also for "Monday Morning" by Helen Wing, which is republished with the permission of the copyright owners; and to D. Appleton-Century Company for the following from St. Nicholas, "A Kindergarten Orator," "A Word to the Wise," "A Surprise," and "My Lady Fair."

Contents

Contents

IF YOU ARE GOING TO MAKE A SPEECH

POEMS FOR SCHOOL PROGRAMS

POEMS FOR HOLIDAY PROGRAMS

CHRISTMAS POEMS

MAY DAY POEMS

MOTHER'S DAY POEMS

HALLOWE'EN POEMS

THANKSGIVING POEMS

PATRIOTIC POEMS

Contents

CHILDREN'S DAY AND RALLY DAY POEMS

PRAYERS AND BLESSINGS

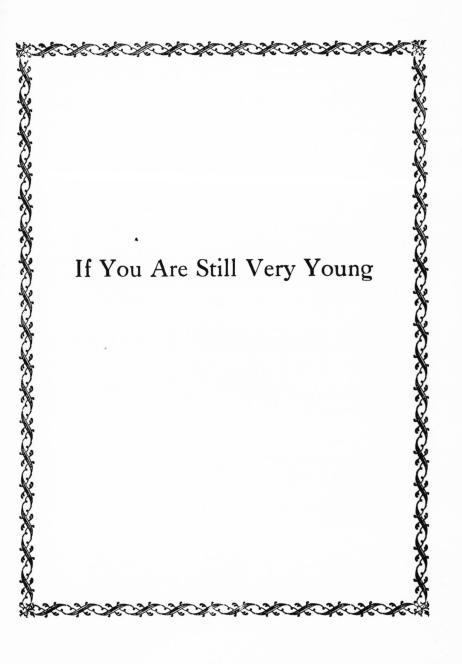

If You Are Still Very Young

I'M GLAD

I'm glad the sky is painted blue,
And earth is painted green,
With such a lot of nice fresh air
All sandwiched in between.

—*Nursery Rhyme*

HAPPY THOUGHT

The world is so full of a number of things,
I'm sure we should all be as happy as kings.

—*Robert Louis Stevenson*

THE CLOCK

Tick, tock, tick, tock,
Merrily sings the clock;
It's time for work,
It's time for play,
So it sings throughout the day.
Tick, tock, tick, tock,
Merrily sings the clock.

—*Nursery Rhyme*

UPON A GREAT BLACK HORSE-ILY

Upon a great black horse-ily
A man came riding cross-ily;
A lady out did come-ily,
Said she, " No one's at home-ily,

" But only little people-y,
Who've gone to bed to sleep-ily."
The rider on his horse-ily
Said to the lady cross-ily,

" But are they bad or good-ily?
I want it understood-ily."
" Oh, they act bad and bold-ily,
And don't do what they're told-ily."

" Good-bye! " said he, " dear ma'am-ily,
I've nothing for your family."
And scampered off like mouse-ily
Away, way from the house-ily.
               —*Nursery Rhyme*

" IT "

A wee little worm in a hickory-nut
    Sang, happy as he could be,—
" O, I live in the heart of the whole round world,
    And it all belongs to me! "
                    —James Whitcomb Riley

PRECOCIOUS PIGGY

Where are you going to, you little pig?
" I'm leaving my mother, I'm growing so big! "
        So big, young pig,
        So young, so big!
What, leaving your mother, you foolish young
    pig?

Where are you going to, you little pig?
" I've got a new spade, and I'm going to dig! "
        To dig, little pig!
        A little pig dig!
Well, I never saw a pig with a spade that could
    dig!

Where are you going to, you little pig?
" Why, I'm going to have a nice ride in a gig! "
        In a gig, little pig!
        What, a pig in a gig!
Well, I never yet saw a pig ride in a gig!

Where are you going to, you little pig?
" Why, I'm going to the Ball to dance a fine jig! "
A jig, little pig!
A pig dance a jig!
Well, I never before saw a pig dance a jig!

Where are you going to, you little pig?
" I'm going to the Fair to run a fine rig! "
A rig, little pig!
A pig run a rig!
Well, I never before saw a pig run a rig!

Where are you going to, you little pig?
" I'm going to the Barber's to buy me a wig! "
A wig, little pig!
A pig in a wig!
Why, whoever before saw a pig in a wig!

Where are you going to, you little pig?
" The Butcher is coming, I've grown so big! "
The Butcher! Poor pig!
Are you grown so big?
Well, I think it high time, then, you hop to the
twig!

—*Thomas Hood*

POLITENESS

Hearts, like doors, will ope with ease
  To very, very little keys,
And don't forget that two of these
  Are " Thank you, sir," and " If you please."
                                    —*Unknown*

ONE MISTY, MOISTY MORNING

One misty, moisty morning,
  When cloudy was the weather,
I chanced to meet an old man
  Clothed all in leather.
He began to compliment,
  And I began to grin,—
" How do you do? " and " How do you do? "
  And " How do you do? " again.
                              —*Nursery Rhyme*

MONDAY MORNING

In the tub on Monday morning
All my dolly's dresses go;
There they dance among the bubbles
Till they're white as snow.
When I squeeze the water out
And hang them up to dry,
They wave their arms excitedly
To people passing by.

—Helen Wing

PUDDING AND MILK

Two little bowls
   Round and white,
Two little spoons
   Silver bright.
Two little stools
   Side by side,
Two little girls,
   Mother's pride.
Pudding and milk
   Mothers know
Is just what makes
   Little girls grow!

        —Unknown

MIX A PANCAKE

Mix a pancake,
Stir a pancake,
    Pop it in the pan.

Fry a pancake,
Toss a pancake,
    Catch it if you can.
    —*Christina G. Rossetti*

PEENY-PEN-PONE

Peeny-Pen, Peeny-Pen, Peeny-Pen-Pone
Is a little old woman who lives all alone!
Her little brown house is on Reeny-Ren-Road,
It looks like a little round Tippity Toad!
In the little brown house is a little brown room,
In the room is a chair and a bed and a broom,
And a little brown table; I think that is all,
Except for a cupboard that stands by the wall,
And a little red fire that burns in the grate,
And a little blue clock that ticks early and late.
" Peeny-Pen, what do you do every day,
For you live all alone and are too old to play? "
" I rise in the morning, I rise with the sun,
I poke my red fire and I make Sally Lunn!
And then I go out and I feed my pink pig
On bees and on beetles to make him grow big!
And then I go round to my little front gate,
And pat my dog Pim on his little brown pate!

And then I go gather a hundred green peas,
And cook them for dinner as hot as I please!
And right after dinner I lock up my house,
And walk down the road in my Sunday-best
blouse;
Down Reeny-Ren-Road and afar, far off,
To call on my little friend Nimmo, the Dwarf.
And Nimmo and I, whatever the weather,
Go faring in Weeny-Wen-Woodland together.
And the rest I can't tell—it's a Secret, you see,
'Tween the Weeny-Wen-Fairies, and Nimmo
and me!
And at eight by the clock I am back in my room,
A-sweeping it out with my little brown broom!
Then I sit by the fire to warm my old head,
And at ten by the clock I jump into bed! "
Thus spoke the old woman that lives all alone,
Peeny-Pen, Peeny-Pen, Peeny-Pen-Pone!

—*Laura Campbell*

BABY SEEDS

In a milkweed cradle,
  Snug and warm,
Baby seeds are hiding,
  Safe from harm.
Open wide the cradle,
  Hold it high!
Come, Mr. Wind,
  Help them fly.

            —Unknown

FARM VOICES

Here's the drover with his cattle,
   Clear the way, oh! clear the way!
Oh! the noisy, noisy creatures,
   Listen now to what they say.
The cows are lowing " Moo, moo, moo! "
The sheep are bleating " Baa, baa, baa! "
The pigs are grunting " Ugh, ugh, ugh! "
And the donkey, with long, long ears,
   Says " Hee-haw, hee-haw, hee-haw! "

Here's the farmer with his poultry,
   Clear the way, oh! clear the way!
Oh! the noisy, noisy creatures,
   Listen now to what they say.
The geese are hissing " Sss,—sss,—sss! "
The hens are calling " Cluck, cluck, cluck! "
The chickens answer " Peep, peep, peep! "
And the rooster, with the gay red comb,
   Says " Cock-a-doodle-doo! "

Everywhere the birds are flying,
  Blithe and gay, oh! blithe and gay.
Merrily their notes are ringing,
  Listen now to what they say.
The robins warble "Chirrup, chirrup, chir-
  rup!"
The sparrows twitter "Tweet, tweet, tweet!"
The pigeons murmur "Coo, coo, coo!"
And the bobolink, so full of joy,
  Sings "Bob-o'-link, bob-o'-link, bob-o'-link!"
                              —*Emilie Poulsson*

THE LITTLE BIRD

Once I saw a little bird
  Come hop, hop, hop;
So I cried, " Little bird,
  Will you stop, stop, stop? "
And went to the window
  To say " How do you do? "
But he shook his little tail
  And away he flew.
            —*Nursery Rhyme*

TIME TO RISE

A birdie with a yellow bill
  Hopped upon the window sill,
Cocked his shiny eye and said:
  " Ain't you 'shamed, you sleepy-head? "
            —*Robert Louis Stevenson*

WHAT DOES LITTLE BIRDIE SAY?

What does the little birdie say
In her nest at peep of day?
Let me fly, says little birdie,
Mother, let me fly away.
Birdie, rest a little longer,
Till the little wings are stronger.
So she rests a little longer,
Then she flies away.

What does the little baby say,
In her bed at peep of day?
Baby says, like little birdie,
Let me rise and fly away.
Baby, sleep a little longer,
Till the little limbs are stronger,
If she sleeps a little longer,
Baby too shall fly away.

—Alfred Tennyson

SINGING

Of speckled eggs the birdie sings,
    And nests among the trees;
The sailor sings of ropes and things
    In ships upon the seas.

The children sing in far Japan,
    The children sing in Spain;
The organ with the organ man
    Is singing in the rain.

—*Robert Louis Stevenson*

In go-cart so tiny
My sister I drew.

AROUND THE WORLD

In go-cart so tiny
    My sister I drew;
And I've promised to draw her
    The wide world through.

We have not yet started—
    I own it with sorrow—
Because our trip's always
    Put off till tomorrow.
                        —*Kate Greenaway*

A LITTLE COCK SPARROW

A little cock sparrow sat on a green tree,
And he chirrup'd, and chirrup'd, so merry was
he.
But a naughty boy came with his wee bow and ar-
row,
Determined to shoot this little cock sparrow.

" This little cock sparrow shall make me a stew,"
Said this naughty boy, " Yes, and a little pie, too."
" Oh, no!" said the sparrow, " I *won't* make a
stew."
So he fluttered his wings, and away he flew.

—*Nursery Rhyme*

JOAN

Here am I,
Little jumping Joan,
When nobody's with me,
I'm always alone.

Hinx, minx! the old witch winks,
The fat begins to fry;
There's nobody at home but jumping Joan
Father, mother and I!
—*Nursery Rhyme*

COCK ROBIN AND JENNY WREN

'Twas on a merry time,
　　When Jenny Wren was young,
So neatly as she danced
　　And so neatly as she sung,
Robin Redbreast lost his heart—
　　He was a gallant bird,
He doffed his cap to Jenny Wren,
　　Requesting to be heard.

" My dearest Jenny Wren,
　　If you will but be mine,
You shall dine on cherry pie,
　　And drink nice currant wine.
I'll dress you like a goldfinch,
　　Or like a peacock gay,
So if you'll have me, Jenny dear,
　　Let us appoint the day."

Jenny blushed behind her fan,
   And thus declared her mind—
" So let it be tomorrow, Rob,
   I'll take your offer kind.
Cherry pie is very good,
   And so is currant wine,
But I will wear my plain brown gown,
   And never dress too fine."

Robin Redbreast got up early
   All at the break of day,
And flew to Jenny Wren's house,
   And sang a roundelay.
He sang of Robin Redbreast
   And pretty Jenny Wren,
And when he came unto the end
   He then began again.
                    —*Old Nursery Song*

THE LIGHT-HEARTED FAIRY

Oh, who is so merry, so merry, heigh ho!
As the light-hearted fairy? heigh ho,
Heigh ho!
He dances and sings
To the sound of his wings
With a hey and a heigh and a ho!

Oh, who is so merry, so airy, heigh ho!
As the light-hearted fairy? heigh ho,
Heigh ho!
His nectar he sips
From the primroses' lips
With a hey and a heigh and a ho!

Oh, who is so merry, so merry, heigh ho!
As the light-footed fairy? heigh ho!
Heigh ho!

The night is his noon
And his sun is the moon,
With a hey and a heigh and a ho!
—*Unknown*

GRASSHOPPER GREEN

Grasshopper green is a comical chap;
   He lives on the best of fare.
Bright little trousers, jacket, and cap,
   These are his summer wear.
Out in the meadow he loves to go,
   Playing away in the sun;
It's hopperty, skipperty, high and low,
   Summer's the time for fun.

Grasshopper green has a quaint little house;
   It's under the hedge so gay.
Grandmother Spider, as still as a mouse,
   Watches him over the way.
Gladly he's calling the children, I know,
   Out in the beautiful sun;
It's hopperty, skipperty, high and low,
   Summer's the time for fun.

—Unknown

MY FEET

My feet, they haul me Round the House,
    They Hoist me up the Stairs;
I only have to Steer them and
    They Ride me Everywheres.
                    —Gelett Burgess

A MILLION LITTLE DIAMONDS

A million little diamonds
   Twinkled on the trees,
And all the little maidens said:
   " A jewel if you please! "

But while they held their hands outstretched,
   To catch the diamonds gay,
A million little sunbeams came,
   And stole them all away.

                      —Unknown

WHISKY FRISKY

Whisky Frisky,
Hippity hop,
Up he goes
To the tree top!

Whirly, twirly,
Round and round,
Down he scampers
To the ground.

Furly, curly,
What a tail!
Tall as a feather,
Broad as a sail!

Where's his supper?
In the shell.
Snappy, cracky,
Out it fell.

—Unknown

FIVE LITTLE CHICKENS

Said the first little chicken,
With a queer little squirm,
" Oh, I wish I could find
A fat little worm! "

Said the next little chicken,
With an odd little shrug,
" Oh, I wish I could find
A fat little bug! "

Said the third little chicken,
With a sharp little squeal,
" Oh, I wish I could find
Some nice yellow meal! "

Said the fourth little chicken,
With a small sigh of grief,
" Oh, I wish I could find
A green little leaf! "

Said the fifth little chicken,
With a faint little moan,
" Oh, I wish I could find
A wee gravel-stone! "

" Now, see here," said the mother,
From the green garden-patch,
" If you want any breakfast,
You must come and scratch."

—Unknown

THE DUCK AND THE KANGAROO

" Please give me a ride on your back,"
    Said the duck to the kangaroo:
" I would sit quite still and say nothing but
    ' Quack!'
    The whole of the long day through;
And we'd go to the Dee, and the Jelly Bo Lee,
    Over the land and over the sea:
Please take me a ride! Oh, do! "
    Said the duck to the kangaroo.

                —*Edward Lear*

POPPING CORN SONG

Bring a yellow ear of corn, then rub, rub, rub,
Till the kernels rattle off the nub, nub, nub;
Put them in a popper made of wire, wire, wire,
And shake the little popper o'er the fire, fire, fire!
If you find them getting lively, give a shake,
    shake, shake,
And a very merry clatter they will make, make,
    make.
Soon you'll hear the heated grains go pop, pop,
    pop,
All about the little popper as they hop, hop, hop!
When you see the yellow corn turn white, white,
    white,
You may know the popping is just right, right,
    right.
When the popper gets too full, you may know,
    know, know,

That the fire has changed your corn to snow, snow, snow!

Turn the snow into a dish, for it's done, done, done,

Then pass it round and eat it,—oh what fun, fun, fun!

—*Unknown*

And shake the little popper o'er the fire, fire, fire.

THE OWL AND THE PUSSY-CAT

The owl and the pussy-cat went to sea
   In a beautiful pea-green boat:
They took some honey, and plenty of money
   Wrapped up in a five-pound note.
The owl looked up to the stars above,
   And sang to a small guitar,
" O lovely Pussy, O Pussy, my love,
What a beautiful Pussy you are,
         You are,
         You are!
What a beautiful Pussy you are! "

Pussy said to the Owl, " You elegant fowl,
   How charmingly sweet you sing!
Oh! let us be married; too long we have tarried;
   But what shall we do for a ring? "
They sailed away, for a year and a day,
   To the land where the bong-tree grows;

And there in a wood a Piggy-wig stood,
  With a ring at the end of his nose,
        His nose,
        His nose,
With a ring at the end of his nose.

" Dear Pig, are you willing to sell for one shil-
      ling
  Your ring? " Said the Piggy, " I will."
So they took it away, and were married next day
  By the Turkey who lives on the hill.
They dined on mince and slices of quince,
  Which they ate with a runcible spoon;
And hand in hand, on the edge of the sand,
  They danced by the light of the moon,
        The moon,
        The moon,
They danced by the light of the moon.

                              —*Edward Lear*

LAWKAMERCYME

There was an old woman, so I've heard tell,
She went to the market, her eggs to sell;
She went to the market on market day,
And she fell asleep on the King's highway.

Along came a pedlar; his name, it was Stout,
And he cut all her petticoats, all round about!
He cut all her petticoats up to her knees,
Which made the old woman to shiver and freeze.

When the old woman first did awake,
She 'gan to shiver, she 'gan to shake,
She 'gan to wonder, she 'gan to cry:
" Lawkamercyme! This is none of I!

" But if it be I, as I do hope it be,
I have a little dog at home and he'll know me;
If it be I, he'll wag his little tail,
And if it be not I, he'll bark and he'll wail! "

Home went the old woman, all in the dark,
Up got the little dog, and he began to bark;
He began to bark, so she began to cry,
" Lawkamercyme! This is none of I! "
                                   —*Old English Rhyme*

NURSERY TALES

There was an old man,
And he had a calf,
  And that's half;
He took him out of the stall,
And tied him to the wall,
  And that's all.

I'll tell you a story
About Jack-a-Nory,
  And now my story's begun;
I'll tell you another
About his brother,
  And now my story's done.

HOBBLEDY HOPS

Hobbledy Hops,
He made some tops
  Out of the morning-glory;
He used the seed,—
He did indeed,
  And that's the end of my story.
—Nursery Rhyme

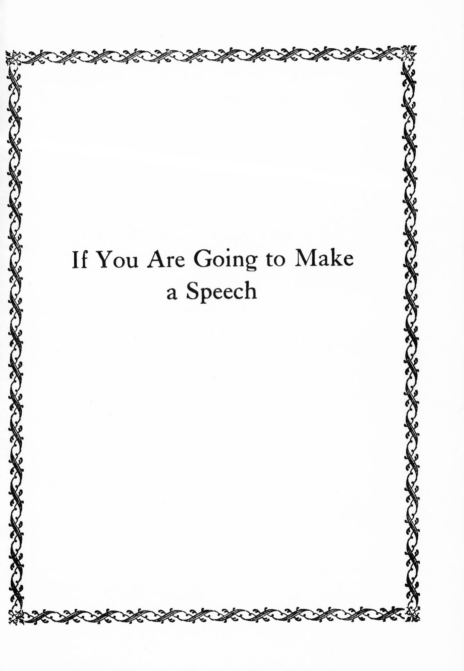

If You Are Going to Make
a Speech

OPENING ADDRESS

Kind friends, we welcome you today
    With songs of merry glee;
Your loving smiles we strive to win,
    Each face we love to see.

Sweet welcomes then to one and all,
    And may your smiles approve;
And may we never miss the light
    Of faces that we love.

                        —*Unknown*

ONLY FIVE

I'm such a very little girl,
    I'm only five years old.
I hope that none who hears me speak
    Will think I am too bold.

                        —*Unknown*

A SPEECH

Pray, how shall I, a little lad,
    In speaking, make a figure?
I hope you'll just be patient
    And wait until I'm bigger.
             —*Unknown*

GREETINGS!

Greetings, friends, we welcome you!
Soon you'll see what we can do;
If you like our little play,
Please come again another day.
             —*Clare Hough Babbitt*

A KINDERGARTEN ORATOR

I would like to speak,
But I don't know how;
So I'll stop right here
And make my bow.
—*Julia H. May*

A SPEECH

My papa sometimes scolds and says,
I'm always in a fidget;
But mamma says, I keep quite still
For such a little midget.

My teacher said today, she thought
That it was very smart
For such a little thing as I
To learn a speech by heart.
—*Unknown*

SCHOOL GREETING

I greet you now, my schoolmates dear,
With best of wishes and loving cheer;
With peace and love within my heart,
I bid you share my joy to part.

Now that our study time is past,
We'll run, and play, and grow so fast,
That when our school begins once more
We'll study better than before.

When playing 'mid the summer flowers,
We'll not forget our schoolday hours;
I hope to meet you, one and all,
When school commences in the fall.

—*G. Scott*

A BOY'S SPEECH

Some of the boys in our school,
   Whose elbows I can't reach,
Are ten times more afraid than I
   To rise and make a speech.

I guess they think that some one—
   Perhaps a girl their age—
May laugh and criticize their looks
   When they come on the stage.

I'm not upset nor stage-struck—
   Could do this every day—
And now I'd make my speech except
   I can't think what to say.

                —*Unknown*

CLOSING ADDRESS

You've seen our entertainment through,
We've tried to please each one of you—
And if we've failed in any part,
Lay it to *head* and not to *heart;*
We thank you for your presence here,
With kindly smiles our work to cheer,
Our youthful zeal you do inspire
To set our mark a little higher—
But there's much more than words can tell,—
So thanking you we'll say—farewell!

—Unknown

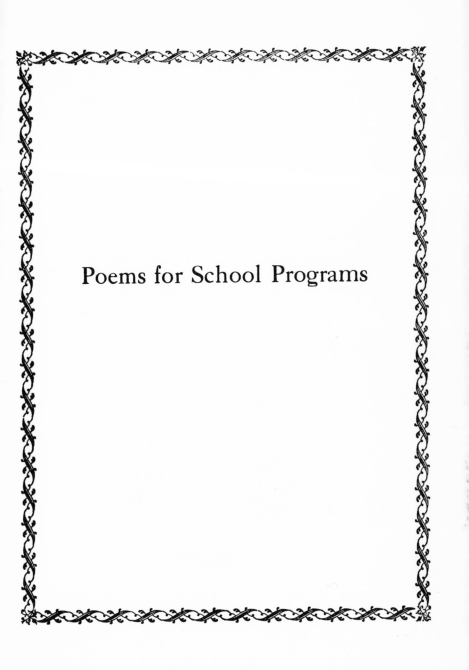

Poems for School Programs

THE VOWELS: A RIDDLE

We are little airy creatures,
All of different voice and features;
One of us in glass is set,
One of us you'll find in jet.
T'other you may see in tin,
And the fourth a box within.
If the fifth you should pursue,
It can never fly from you.
—Jonathan Swift

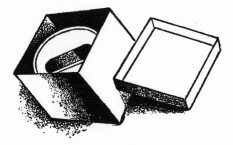

GRAMMAR IN A NUTSHELL

Three little words you often see
Are articles—*a, an,* and *the.*

A noun's the name of anything,
As *school,* or *garden, hoop,* or *swing.*

Adjectives tell the kind of noun,
As *great, small, pretty, white* or *brown.*

Instead of nouns the pronouns stand—
Her head, *his* face, *your* arm, *my* hand.

Verbs tell of something being done—
To *read, count, laugh, sing, jump,* or *run.*

How things are done the adverbs tell,
As *slowly, quickly, ill* or *well.*

Conjunctions join the words together,
As men *and* women, wind *or* weather.

[66]

The preposition stands before
A noun, as *in* or *through* the door.

The interjection shows surprise,
As *oh!* how pretty! *ah!* how wise!

The whole are called nine parts of speech,
Which reading, writing, speaking, teach.

                              —Unknown

ARITHMETIC

Multiplication is vexation,
   Division is as bad;
The Rule of Three perplexes me
And Practice drives me mad.
—Unknown

LIMERICK

There was an old man who said, " Do
Tell me *how* I should add two and two?
   I think more and more
   That it makes about four—
But I fear that is almost too few."
—Edward Lear

You should say, "To *whom! To whom!*"

A WORD TO THE WISE

Little owlet in the glen,
  I'm ashamed of you;
You are ungrammatical
  In speaking as you do.
You should say, " To *whom!* To *whom!* "
  Not, " To *who!* To *who!* "

Your small friend, Miss Katy-did,
  May be green, 'tis true,
But you never hear *her* say,
  " Katy-*do!* She *do!* "
                    —*Louise M. Laughton*

A SURPRISE

When the donkey saw the zebra
   He began to switch his tail.
" Well, I never!" was his comment;
   " Here's a mule that's been to jail!"
               —*Malcolm Douglas*

THE ICHTHYOSAURUS

There once was an Ichthyosaurus
Who lived when the earth was all porous,
But he fainted with shame
When he first heard his name,
And departed a long time before us.
                    —*Unknown*

THE OSTRICH IS A SILLY BIRD

The ostrich is a silly bird,
  With scarcely any mind.
He often runs so very fast,
  He leaves himself behind.

And when he gets there, has to stand
  And hang about till night,
Without a blessed thing to do
  Until he comes in sight.
  —*Mary E. Wilkins Freeman*

I'D RATHER HAVE FINGERS
THAN TOES

I'd rather have Fingers than Toes;
I'd rather have Ears than a Nose;
    And as for my Hair,
    I'm glad it's All There;
I'll be Awfully Sad when it Goes!
              —Gelett Burgess

THE PURPLE COW

I never saw a Purple Cow,
    I never hope to see one;
But I can tell you, anyhow,
    I'd rather see than be one.
              —Gelett Burgess

THE LITTLE TURTLE

There was a little turtle,
    He lived in a box,
He swam in a puddle,
    He climbed on the rocks.

He snapped at a mosquito,
    He snapped at a flea,
He snapped at a minnow,
    And he snapped at me.

He caught the mosquito,
    He caught the flea,
He caught the minnow,
    But he didn't catch me.
                    —*Vachel Lindsay*

A QUARREL

There's a knowing little proverb
  From the sunny land of Spain,
But in the north and in the south
  Its meaning's clear and plain.
Lock it up within your heart—
  Neither lose nor lend it:
Two it takes to make a quarrel—
  One can always end it.

Try it well in every way,
  Still you'll find it true.
In a fight without a foe,
  Pray, what could you do?
If but one shall span the breach,
  He will quickly mend it.
Two it takes to make a quarrel—
  One can always end it.

                    —*Unknown*

THE CITY MOUSE AND THE GARDEN MOUSE

The city mouse lives in a house;—
  The garden nouse lives in a bower,
He's friendly with the frogs and toads,
  And sees the pretty plants in flower.

The city mouse eats bread and cheese;—
  The garden mouse eats what he can;
We will not grudge him seeds and stocks,
  Poor little timid furry man.

           —*Christina G. Rossetti*

THE SWING

How do you like to go up in a swing,
   Up in the air so blue?
Oh, I do think it the pleasantest thing
   Ever a child can do!

Up in the air and over the wall,
   Till I can see so wide,
River and trees and cattle and all
   Over the countryside—

Till I look down on the garden green,
   Down on the roof so brown—
Up in the air I go flying again,
   Up in the air and down!

               —*Robert Louis Stevenson*

Up in the air I go flying again,
Up in the air and down!

FOOLISH FLOWERS

We've Foxgloves in our garden;
  How careless they must be
To leave their gloves out hanging
  Where everyone can see!

And Bachelors leave their Buttons
  In the same careless way,
If I should do the same with mine,
  What would my Mother say?

We've lots of Larkspurs in the yard—
  Larks only fly and sing—
Birds surely don't need spurs because
  They don't ride anything!

And as for Johnny-Jump-Ups—
  I saw a hornet light
On one of them the other day,
  He didn't jump a mite!

                —*Rupert Sargent Holland*

THE CATS' TEA-PARTY

Five little pussy-cats, invited out to tea,

Cried: "Mother, let us go—Oh, do! for good
we'll surely be.

We'll wear our bibs and hold our things as you
have shown us how—

Spoons in right paws, cups in left—and make a
pretty bow;

We'll always say, 'Yes, if you please,' and 'Only
half of that.'"

"Then go, my darling children," said the happy
Mother Cat.

The five little pussy-cats went out that night to
tea,

Their heads were smooth and glossy, their tails
were swinging free,

They held their things as they had learned, and
tried to be polite,—

With snowy bibs beneath their chins they were a
   pretty sight.
But, alas, for manners beautiful, and coats as soft
   as silk!
The moment that the little kits were asked to take
   some milk,
They dropped their spoons, forgot to bow, and—
   oh, what do you think?
They put their noses in their cups and all began
   to drink!
Yes, every naughty little kit set up a miou for
   more,
Then knocked the tea-cups over, and scampered
   through the door!

                    —*Frederick Edward Weatherly*

SEVEN TIMES ONE

There's no dew left on the daisies and clover,
　　There's no rain left in heaven;
I've said my " seven times " over and over—
　　Seven times one are seven.

I am old! so old I can write a letter;
　　My birthday lessons are done:
The lambs play always, they know no better;
　　They are only one times one.

O Moon! in the night I have seen you sailing,
　　And shining so round and low;
You were bright! ah, bright! but your light is
　　　　failing;
　　You are nothing now but a bow.

You Moon! have you done something wrong in
　　　　heaven,
　　That God has hidden your face?

I hope if you have, you will soon be forgiven,
  And shine again in your place.

O velvet Bee! You're a dusty fellow,
  You've powdered your legs with gold;
O brave marsh Mary-buds, rich and yellow!
  Give me your money to hold.

O Columbine! open your folded wrapper
  Where two twin turtle-doves dwell;
O Cuckoo-pint! toll me the purple clapper,
  That hangs in your clear green bell.

And show me your nest with the young ones in
        it—
  I will not steal them away,
I am old! You may trust me, Linnet, Linnet,—
  I am seven times one today.

                          —*Jean Ingelow*

WHITE BUTTERFLIES

Fly, white butterflies, out to sea,
Frail, pale wings for the wind to try,
Small white wings that we scarce can see,
     Fly!

Some fly light as a laugh of glee,
Some fly soft as a long, low sigh;
All to the haven where each would be,
     Fly!

—Algernon Charles Swinburne

NIGHT

Stars over snow,
   And in the west a planet
Swinging below a star—
   Look for a lovely thing and you will find it,
It is not far—
   It never will be far.

—Sara Teasdale

THE CHILD AND THE FAIRIES

The woods are full of fairies!
　　The trees are all alive;
The river overflows with them,
　　See how they dip and dive!
What funny little fellows!
　　What dainty little dears!
They dance and leap, and prance and peep,
　　And utter fairy cheers!

I'd like to tame a fairy,
　　To keep it on a shelf,
To see it wash its little face,
　　And dress its little self.
I'd teach it pretty manners,
　　It always should say " Please ";
And then you know I'd make it sew,
　　And curtsey with its knees!
　　　　　　　　　—Unknown

FAIRY BREAD

Come up here, O dusty feet!
Here is fairy bread to eat.
Here in my retiring room,
   Children you may dine
On the golden smell of broom
   And the shade of pine;
And when you have eaten well,
Fairy stories hear and tell.

—Robert Louis Stevenson

GOOD NIGHT AND GOOD MORNING

A fair little girl sat under a tree,
Sewing as long as her eyes could see;
Then smoothed her work and folded it right,
And said, " Dear work, good night, good
    night! "

Such a number or rooks came over her head,
Crying, " Caw! Caw! " on their way to bed,
She said, as she watched their curious flight,
" Little black things, good night, good night! "

The horses neighed, and the oxen lowed,
The sheep's " Bleat! Bleat! " came over the road;
All seeming to say, with a quiet delight,
" Good little girl, good night, good night! "

She did not say to the sun, " Good night! "
Though she saw him there like a ball of light;

For she knew he had God's time to keep
All over the world, and never could sleep.

The tall pink foxglove bowed his head;
The violets curtsied, and went to bed;
And good little Lucy tied up her hair,
And said, on her knees, her favorite prayer.

And while on her pillow she softly lay,
She knew nothing more till again it was day;
And all things said to the beautiful sun,
" Good morning, good morning! Our work is
    begun."

—*Lord Houghton*

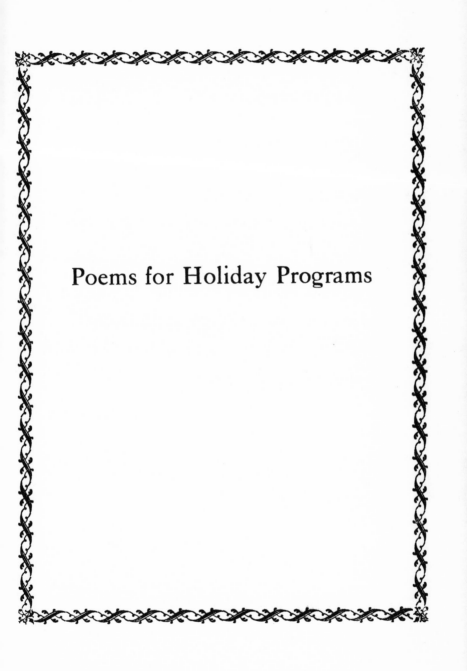

Poems for Holiday Programs

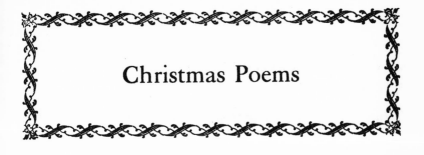

Christmas Poems

MY GIFT

What can I give Him
Poor as I am;
If I were a shepherd,
I would give Him a lamb.
If I were a wise man,
I would do my part.
But what can I give Him?
I will give Him my heart.

—*Christina G. Rossetti*

CRADLE HYMN

Away in a manger, no crib for a bed,
The little Lord Jesus laid down his sweet head.
The stars in the bright sky looked down where he
     lay—
The little Lord Jesus asleep on the hay.

The cattle are lowing, the baby awakes,
But little Lord Jesus, no crying he makes.
I love thee, Lord Jesus! look down from the sky,
And stay by my cradle till morning is nigh.

                          —*Martin Luther*

EARTH AND SKY

(They talk to each other on Christmas Eve)

EARTH	Oh Sky, you look so drear!
SKY	Oh Earth, you look so bare!
EARTH	How chilly you appear!
SKY	How empty you lie there!

SKY	My winds blow icy cold.
EARTH	My flowers have gone from me.
SKY	Yet I've one star of gold.
EARTH	And I have one green tree.
SKY	I'll set my star on high
	Alone in its own light
	For any child to spy
	Who wakes on Christmas Night.
EARTH	I'll hang my tree with toys,
	Like fruit and flowers gay,
	For little girls and boys
	To pick on Christmas Day.

THEY Then let the soft snow fall,
SAY TO- And let the cold wind blow!
GETHER: We have in spite of all
A pretty thing to show.

Yes, Christmas Eve and Morn
We'll show our pretty thing
To every baby born
Of Beggar-man or King.

EARTH Oh Sky, you look so clear!
SKY Oh Earth, you look so fair!
EARTH How bright your star shines here.
SKY How green your Tree grows there.

—*Eleanor Farjeon*

CHRISTMAS BELLS

" Are you waking? " shout the breezes
  To the tree-tops waving high,
" Don't you hear the happy tidings
  Whispered to the earth and sky?
Have you caught them in your dreaming,
  Brook and rill in snowy dells?
Do you know the joy we bring you
  In the merry Christmas bells?
  Ding, dong! ding, dong, Christmas bells!

" Are you waking, flowers that slumber
  In the deep and frosty ground?
Do you hear what we are breathing
  To the listening world around?
For we bear the sweetest story
  That the glad year ever tells:
How He loved the little children,—
  He who brought the Christmas bells!
  Ding, dong! ding, dong, Christmas bells! "

          —*George Cooper*

A CHRISTMAS CAROL

God rest ye merry, gentlemen; let nothing you
dismay,
For Jesus Christ, our Saviour, was born on
Christmas Day.

The dawn rose red o'er Bethlehem, the stars
shone through the gray,
When Jesus Christ, our Saviour, was born on
Christmas Day.

God rest ye, little children; let nothing you af-
fright,
For Jesus Christ, our Saviour, was born this
happy night;

Along the hills of Galilee the white flocks sleep-
ing lay,
When Christ, the Child of Nazareth, was born
on Christmas Day.

—Dinah M. Mulock Craik

ONCE IN ROYAL DAVID'S CITY

Once in royal David's city
    Stood a lowly cattle shed,
Where a Mother laid her baby
    In a manger for His bed;
Mary was that Mother mild,
Jesus Christ her little child.

He came down to earth from heaven,
    Who is God and Lord of all,
And His shelter was a stable,
    And His cradle was a stall,
With the poor, and mean, and lowly
Lived on earth, our Saviour Holy.

Not in that poor lowly stable,
    With the oxen standing by,
We shall see Him; but in heaven,
    Set at God's right hand on high,

When like stars His children crowned,
All in white shall wait around.

—Cecil Frances Alexander

CHRISTMAS CAROL

God bless the master of this house,
   The mistress also,
And all the little children,
   That round the table go,
And all your kin and kinsmen
   That dwell both far and near;
I wish you a Merry Christmas
   And a Happy New Year.

—Old Rhyme

SANTA CLAUS

Little fairy snowflakes
   Dancing in the flue;
Old Mr. Santa Claus,
   What is keeping you?
Twilight and firelight
   Shadows come and go;
Merry chime of sleigh-bells
   Twinkling through the snow.
Mother's knitting stockings,
   Pussy's got the ball.
Don't you think that Christmas
   Is pleasantest of all?

               —*Unknown*

SANTA CLAUS

He comes in the night! He comes in the night!
　　He softly, silently comes;
While the little brown heads on the pillows so
　　　　white
　　Are dreaming of bugles and drums.
He cuts through the snow like a ship through the
　　　　foam,
　　While the white flakes around him whirl;
Who tells him I know not, but he findeth the
　　　　home
　　Of each good little boy and girl.

His sleigh it is long, and deep, and wide;
　　It will carry a host of things,
While dozens of drums hang over the side,
　　With the sticks sticking under the strings.
And yet not the sound of a drum is heard,
　　Not a bugle blast is blown,

As he mounts to the chimney-top like a bird,
  And drops to the hearth like a stone.

The little red stockings he silently fills,
  Till the stockings will hold no more;
The bright little sleds for the great snow hills
  Are quickly set down on the floor.
Then Santa Claus mounts to the roof like a bird,
  And glides to his seat in the sleigh;
Not the sound of a bugle or drum is heard
  As he noiselessly gallops away.

—Unknown

CHRISTMAS HEARTH RHYME

Sing we all merrily,
  Christmas is here,
The day we love best
  Of all days in the year.

Bring forth the holly,
  The box and the bay,
Deck out our cottage
  For glad Christmas Day.

Sing we all merrily,
  Draw near the fire,
Sister and brother,
  Grandson and sire.

          —*Old English Song*

THE FIRST CHRISTMAS

Hang up the baby's stocking;
   Be sure you don't forget—
The dear little dimpled darling!
   She ne'er saw Christmas yet;
But I've told her all about it,
   And she opened her big blue eyes,
And I'm sure she understood it,
   She looked so funny and wise.

Dear! what a tiny stocking!
   It doesn't take much to hold
Such little pink toes as baby's
   Away from the frost and cold.
But then, for the baby's Christmas
   It will never do at all;
Why, Santa wouldn't be looking
   For anything half so small.

I know what will do for the baby,
   I've thought of the very best plan—
I'll borrow a stocking of grandma,
   The longest that ever I can;
And you'll hang it by mine, dear mother,
   Right here in the corner, so!
And write a letter to Santa,
   And fasten it on to the toe.

Write, " This is the baby's stocking
   That hangs in the corner here;
You never have seen her, Santa,
   For she only came this year;
But she's just the blessedest baby—
   And now, before you go,
Just cram her stocking with goodies,
   From the top clean down to the toe."

—*Anonymous*

CHRISTMAS GREETING

Sing hey! Sing hey!
For Christmas Day;
Twine mistletoe and holly,
For friendship glows
In winter snows,
And so let's all be jolly.

—*Old Rhyme*

WHAT MY LITTLE BROTHER THINKS!

My little brother is—oh, so funny!
He thinks that a king is made of money,
He thinks little cherubs, overhead,
Hold up the stars to light us to bed.

He thinks little fairies make the clamor
In Grandpa's watch, with a tiny hammer.
He thinks that fairies live in a book,
Or can dance in kettles to frighten Cook.

He thinks the grasshoppers bring molasses,
That a fairy over the bright moon passes.
He thinks my Jack-in-the-box is alive;—
But my little brother is only five.

But the best of all, he is really certain
He once saw Santa Claus through the curtain;
And he thinks Old Santa'll come by and by
On Christmas Eve—and so do I!

—Unknown

A VISIT FROM ST. NICHOLAS

'Twas the night before Christmas, when all
    through the house
Not a creature was stirring, not even a mouse;
The stockings were hung by the chimney with
    care,
In hopes that St. Nicholas soon would be there;
The children were nestled all snug in their beds,
While visions of sugar-plums danced in their
    heads;
And mamma in her 'kerchief, and I in my cap,
Had just settled our brains for a long winter's
    nap,
When out on the lawn there arose such a clatter,
I sprang from the bed to see what was the matter.
Away to the window I flew like a flash,
Tore open the shutters and threw up the sash.
The moon on the breast of the new-fallen snow
Gave the lustre of midday to objects below,

When, what to my wondering eyes should appear,

But a miniature sleigh, and eight tiny reindeer,

With a little old driver, so lively and quick,

I knew in a moment it must be St. Nick.

More rapid than eagles his coursers they came,

And he whistled, and shouted, and called them by name:

"Now, *Dasher!* now, *Dancer!* now, *Prancer* and *Vixen!*

On, *Comet!* on, *Cupid!* on, *Donder* and *Blitzen!*

To the top of the porch! to the top of the wall!

Now dash away! dash away! dash away all!"

As dry leaves that before the wild hurricane fly,

When they meet with an obstacle, mount to the sky,

So up to the house-top the coursers they flew,

With the sleigh full of toys, and St. Nicholas too.

And then, in a twinkling, I heard on the roof

The prancing and pawing of each little hoof.

As I drew in my head, and was turning around,

Down the chimney St. Nicholas came with a
bound.

He was dressed all in fur, from his head to his
foot,

And his clothes were all tarnished with ashes and
soot;

A bundle of toys he had flung on his back,

And he looked like a peddler just opening his
pack.

His eyes—how they twinkled!—his dimples how
merry!

His cheeks were like roses, his nose like a cherry!

His droll little mouth was drawn up like a bow,

And the beard of his chin was as white as the
snow;

The stump of a pipe he held tight in his teeth,

And the smoke it encircled his head like a
wreath;

He had a broad face and a little round belly,

That shook, when he laughed, like a bowlful of
   jelly.
He was chubby and plump, a right jolly old elf,
And I laughed when I saw him, in spite of my-
   self;
A wink of his eye and a twist of his head,
Soon gave me to know I had nothing to dread;
He spoke not a word, but went straight to his
   work,
And filled all the stockings; then turned with a
   jerk,
And laying his finger aside of his nose,
And giving a nod, up the chimney he rose;
He sprang to his sleigh, to his team gave a
   whistle,
And away they all flew like the down of a thistle.
But I heard him exclaim, ere he drove out of
   sight,
" HAPPY CHRISTMAS TO ALL, AND TO
ALL A GOOD-NIGHT! "

—*Dr. Clement C. Moore*

New Year's Poems

THE NEW YEAR

Who comes dancing over the snow,
His soft little feet all bare and rosy?
Open the door though the wild winds blow,
Take the child in and make him cozy.
Take him in and hold him dear,
He is the wonderful glad New Year.
                    —*Dinah M. Mulock Craik*

THE MONTHS

January brings the snow,
Makes our feet and fingers glow.

February brings the rain,
Thaws the frozen lakes again.

March brings breezes sharp and chill,
Shakes the dancing daffodil.

April brings the primrose sweet,
Scatters daisies at our feet.

May brings flocks of pretty lambs,
Sporting round their fleecy dams.

June brings tulips, lilies, roses,
Fills the children's hands with posies.

Hot July brings thunder-showers,
Apricots, and gilly-flowers.

August brings the sheaves of corn;
Then the harvest home is borne.

Warm September brings the fruit;
Sportsmen then begin to shoot.

Brown October brings the pheasant,
Then to gather nuts is pleasant.

Dull November brings the blast—
Hark! the leaves are whirling fast.

Cold December brings the sleet,
Blazing fire, and Christmas treat.
                    —*Sara Coleridge*

THE YEAR

There is a tree of praise and dower
That beareth much of fruit and flower;
Twelve branches has it, spreading wide,
Where two-and-fifty nests abide,
In every nest the birds are seven;
Thankèd be the King of heaven.

—*Unknown*

I SAW THREE SHIPS

I saw three ships come sailing by,
Sailing by, sailing by,
I saw three ships come sailing by,
   On New Year's Day in the morning.

Three pretty girls were in them then,
In them then, in them then,
Three pretty girls were in them then,
   On New Year's Day in the morning.

And one could whistle, and one could sing,
The other play on the violin,
Such joy there was at my wedding,
   On New Year's Day in the morning.
—Mother Goose

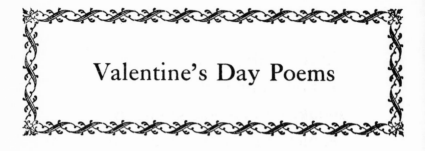

Valentine's Day Poems

MY LADY FAIR

Ah, well-a-day, my lady!
How goes the world with you?
The wee, white clouds are fleecy,
The far-off skies are blue.
I passed the young lambs frisking,
And wondered if they knew
That I had eyes for no one else,
My lady-love, but you!

—Martha Day Fenner

WILL YOU?

Will you be my little wife
 If I ask you? Do!
I'll buy you such a Sunday frock,
 A nice umbrella too.

And you shall have a little hat,
 With such a long white feather,
A pair of gloves, and sandal shoes,
 The softest kind of leather.

And you shall have a tiny house,
 A beehive full of bees,
A little cow, a largish cat,
 And green sage cheese.
     —*Kate Greenaway*

THE PRETTY LITTLE MAIDEN

A pretty little maiden had a pretty little dream,
And a pretty little wedding was its pretty little
theme.
A pretty little bachelor to win her favor tried,
And asked her how she'd like to be his pretty lit-
tle bride!
With some pretty little blushes, and a pretty little
sigh,
And a pretty little glance from her pretty little
eye,
From her pretty little face behind her pretty fan,
She smiled on the proposals of this pretty little
man.
A pretty little wedding ring united them for life,
And this pretty little husband had a pretty little
wife!

—Unknown

THE YOUNG THING

" Where have you been all the day,
  My boy Willy? "
" I've been all the day
Courting of a lady gay :
But, oh! she's too young
To be taken from her mammy."

" What work can she do,
  My boy Willy?
Can she bake and can she brew,
  My boy Willy? "
" She can bake and she can brew,
And she can make our wedding-cake :
But, oh! she's too young
To be taken from her mammy."

" What age may she be? What age may she be?
   My boy Willy? "
" Twice two, twice seven,
Twice ten, twice eleven:
But, oh! she's too young
To be taken from her mammy."

—*Old Song*

ANSWER TO A CHILD'S QUESTION

Do you ask what the birds say? The Sparrow, the Dove,
The Linnet, and Thrush say, " I love and I love! "
In the winter they're silent—the wind is so strong;
What it says, I don't know, but it sings a loud song.
But green leaves, and blossoms, and sunny warm weather,
And singing, and loving—all come back together.
But the Lark is so brimful of gladness and love,
The green fields below him, the blue sky above,
That he sings, and he sings, and forever sings he—
" I love my Love, and my Love loves me! "

—*Samuel Taylor Coleridge*

SOME THINGS THAT EASTER BRINGS

Easter duck and Easter chick,
Easter eggs with chocolate thick.

Easter hats for one and all,
Easter Bunny makes a call!

Happy Easter always brings
Such a lot of pleasant things.
—*Elsie Parrish*

AN EASTER SONG

The mists of Easter morning
  Roll slowly o'er the hills,
The joy of Easter morning,
  The heart of nature thrills.

The songs of birds are calling
  Good people from repose,
To sing of that first Easter
  When Christ the Lord arose.

Upon a thousand altars
  Are flowers of richest bloom,
Proclaiming with sweet voices
  How Jesus left the tomb.

And north and south in anthems,
  And east and west in song,
Through all this happy Eastertide
  His praises shall prolong.

             —T. W. Handford

MEETING THE EASTER BUNNY

On Easter morn at early dawn
    before the cocks were crowing,
I met a bob-tail bunnykin
    and asked where he was going.
" 'Tis in the house and out the house
    a-tipsy, tipsy-toeing,
'Tis round the house and 'bout the house
    a-lightly I am going."
" But what is that of every hue
    you carry in your basket? "
" 'Tis eggs of gold and eggs of blue;
    I wonder that you ask it.
'Tis chocolate eggs and bonbon eggs
    and eggs of red and gray,
For every child in every house
    on bonny Easter Day."
He perked his ears and winked his eye
    and twitched his little nose;

**He shook his tail — what tail he had
and stood up on his toes.**

He shook his tail—what tail he had—
and stood up on his toes.
" I must be gone before the sun;
the East is growing gray;
'Tis almost time for bells to chime."
So he hippety-hopped away.

—*Rowena Bennett*

PIPPA'S SONG

The year's at the spring
And day's at the morn;
Morning's at seven;
The hill-side's dew-pearled;
The lark's on the wing;
The snail's on the thorn;
God's in his heaven—
All's right with the world.

—Robert Browning

SIR ROBIN

Rollicking robin is here again.
What does he care for the April rain?
Care for it? Glad of it! Doesn't he know
That the April rain carries off the snow,
And coaxes out leaves to shadow his nest,
And washes his pretty Easter vest,
And makes the juice of the cherry sweet,
For his hungry little robins to eat?
" Ha! Ha! Ha! " Hear the jolly bird laugh.
" That isn't the best of the story, by half."

—Lucy Larcom

IN THE HEART OF A SEED

In the heart of a seed,
　　Buried deep, so deep,
A dear little plant
　　Lay fast asleep.

" Wake," said the sunshine,
　　" And creep to the light; "
" Wake," said the voice
　　Of the raindrops bright.

The little plant heard,
　　And it rose to see
What the beautiful
　　Outside world might be.
　　　　　　　　—*Kate L. Brown*

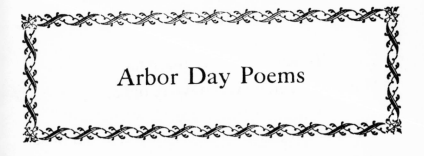

Arbor Day Poems

SEWING

If Mother Nature patches
   The leaves of trees and vines,
I'm sure she does her darning
   With the needles of the pines;
They are so long and slender,
   And somewhere in full view,
She has her threads of cobweb,
   And a thimbleful of dew.

—Unknown

AN ARBOR DAY TREE

" Dear little tree that we plant today,
What will you be when we're old and gray? "

" The savings bank of the squirrel and mouse,
For the robin and wren an apartment house;

The dressing room of the butterfly's ball,
The locust's and katydid's concert hall;

The schoolboy's ladder in pleasant June,
The schoolgirl's tent in the July noon;

And my leaves shall whisper them merrily
A tale of the children who planted me."

—Unknown

CHILD'S SONG IN SPRING

The silver birch is a dainty lady,
  She wears a satin gown;
The elm tree makes the churchyard shady,
  She will not live in town.

The English oak is a sturdy fellow,
  He gets his green coat late;
The willow is smart in a suit of yellow,
  While brown the beech trees wait.

Such a gay green gown God gives the larches—
  As green as He is good!
The hazels hold up their arms for arches
  When Spring rides through the wood.

The chestnut's proud, and the lilac's pretty,
  The poplar's gentle and tall,
But the plane tree's kind to the poor dull city—
  I love him best of all!
                              —*Edith Nesbit*

TREES

The Oak is called the King of Trees,
The Aspen quivers in the breeze,
The Poplar grows up straight and tall,
The Pear-tree spreads along the wall,
The Sycamore gives pleasant shade,
The Willow droops in watery glade,
The Fir-tree useful timber gives,
The Beech amid the forest lives.

—*Sara Coleridge*

OCTOBER'S PARTY

October gave a party;
   The leaves by hundreds came—
The Chestnuts, Oaks, and Maples,
   And leaves of every name.
The Sunshine spread a carpet,
   And everything was grand,
Miss Weather led the dancing,
   Professor Wind the band.

The Chestnuts came in yellow,
   The Oaks in crimson dressed;
The lovely Misses Maple
   In scarlet looked their best;
All balanced to their partners,
   And gaily fluttered by;
The sight was like a rainbow
   New fallen from the sky.

Then, in the rustic hollow,
  At hide-and-seek they played,
The party closed at sundown,
  And everybody stayed.
Professor Wind played louder;
  They flew along the ground;
And then the party ended
  In jolly " hands around."

—*George Cooper*

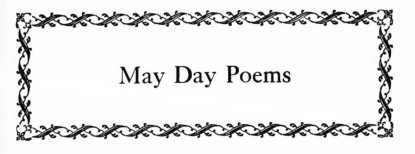

May Day Poems

APRIL AND MAY

April is a laundress
Mixing silver suds
To rinse the lacy dance frocks
Of apple-blossom buds.

May Day is the nursemaid
Who looks the flowers over
And ties their little bonnets
On the buttercup and clover.

—Anne Robinson

MAY DAY

Good morning, lords and ladies, it is the first of
    May;
We hope you'll view our garland, it is so sweet
    and gay.

The cuckoo sings in April, the cuckoo sings in
    May,
The cuckoo sings in June, in July she flies away.

The cuckoo drinks cold water to make her sing
    so clear.
And then she sings "Cuckoo! Cuckoo!" for
    three months in the year.

I love my little brother and sister every day,
But I seem to love them better in the merry month
    of May.

—*Old Song*

OXFORDSHIRE CHILDREN'S
MAY SONG

Spring is coming, spring is coming,
  Birdies, build your nest;
Weave together straw and feather,
  Doing each your best.

Spring is coming, spring is coming,
  Flowers are coming too;
Pansies, lilies, daffodillies,
  Now are coming through.

Spring is coming, spring is coming,
  All around is fair;
Shimmer and quiver on the river,
  Joy is everywhere.

We wish you a happy May!
                —*Old English Rhyme*

Mother's Day Poems

MOTHER

Birdies with broken wings
  Hide from each other,
But babies in trouble
  Run home to mother.

—*Unknown*

ONLY ONE MOTHER

Hundreds of stars in the pretty sky,
  Hundreds of shells on the shore together,
Hundreds of birds that go singing by,
  Hundreds of lambs in the sunny weather.

Hundreds of dewdrops to greet the dawn,
  Hundreds of bees in the purple clover,
Hundreds of butterflies on the lawn,
  But only *one mother* the wide world over.

—*George Cooper*

MY MOTHER

When sleep forsook my open eye,
Who was it sang sweet lullaby,
And rocked me that I should not cry?
  My mother.

Who dressed my doll in clothes so gay,
And taught me how to speak and play,
And minded all I had to say?
  My mother.

Who ran to help me when I fell,
And would some pretty story tell,
Or kiss the place to make it well?
  My mother.

And can I ever cease to be
Affectionate and kind to thee,
Who was so very kind to me?
  My mother.

    —Ann Taylor

A CHILD'S THOUGHT OF GOD

They say that God lives very high!
   But if you look above the pines
You cannot see our God. And why?

And if you dig down in the mines
   You never see Him in the gold,
Though from Him all that's glory shines.

God is so good, He wears a fold
   Of heaven and earth across His face—
Like secrets kept, for love untold.

But still I feel that His embrace
   Slides down by thrills, through all things made,
Through sight and sound of every place:

As if my tender mother laid
   On my shut lids, her kisses' pressure,
Half-waking me at night and said,
   "Who kissed you through the dark, dear
     guesser?"
             —*Elizabeth Barrett Browning*

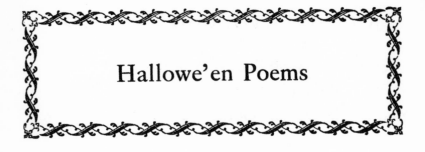

Hallowe'en Poems

HALLOWE'EN

Heyhow for Hallowe'en,
When all the witches are to be seen,
Some in black and some in green,
Heyhow for Hallowe'en.
—*Old Scotch Rhyme*

SOME ONE

Some one came knocking
  At my wee, small door;
Some one came knocking,
  I'm sure—sure—sure;
I listened, I opened,
  I looked to left and right,
But nought there was a-stirring
  In the still dark night;
Only the busy beetle
  Tap-tapping in the wall,
Only from the forest
  The screech-owl's call,
Only the cricket whistling
  While the dewdrops fall,
So I know not who came knocking,
  At all, at all, at all.

—Walter De La Mare

VERY NEARLY

I never *quite* saw fairy folk
  A-dancing in the glade,
Where, just beyond the hollow oak,
  Their broad green rings are laid:
But, while behind that Oak I hid,
One day I very nearly did!

I never *quite* saw mermaids rise
  Above the twilight sea,
When sands, left wet, 'neath sunset skies,
  Are blushing rosily:
But—all alone, those rocks amid—
One day I very nearly did!

I never *quite* saw Goblin Grim,
  Who haunts our lumber room
And pops his head above the rim
  Of that oak chest's deep gloom:
But once—when mother raised the lid—
I very, very nearly did!
                    —*Queenie Scott-Hopper*

A HALLOWE'EN MEETING

I always thought, old witch,
    That you were bad as bad could be,
That if I ever met you
    You would surely frighten me;

I don't believe that you can be
    So very wicked, though,
Or else your owl and pussy cat
    Could never love you so.

        —*George Butler*

Thanksgiving Poems

THANKSGIVING

For each new morning with its light,
    Father, we thank Thee,
For rest and shelter of the night,
    Father, we thank Thee,
For health and food, for love and friends,
For everything Thy goodness sends,
    Father, in heaven, we thank Thee.

                    —Ralph Waldo Emerson

THANKSGIVING TIME

When all the leaves are off the boughs,
  And nuts and apples gathered in,
And cornstalks waiting for the cows,
  And pumpkins safe in barn and bin:

Then mother says: " My children dear,
  The fields are brown and autumn flies;
Thanksgiving Day is very near,
  And we must make Thanksgiving pies! "
                              —*Unknown*

WE THANK THEE

We thank Thee for the sun and rain
That make the fruits, the nuts, the grain;
For food we eat and clothes we wear,
And for our parents' tender care.

We thank Thee for each night's sweet rest,
For friends and those whom we love best;
For long and happy hours to play,
The joy of each new shining day.

We thank Thee for the loveliness
Of nature in her autumn dress,
For sweet sounds that the songbirds bring,
We thank Thee, Lord, for everything.

—Carmen Malone

HARVEST PRAYER

God of the harvest, thanks to Thee
For the grain of the field and the fruit of the tree;
For the pumpkin gold and the apple red,
And all that our hands have harvested;
For the loaded bough and the bulging pod . . .
We thank Thee, God.

—Rowena Bennett

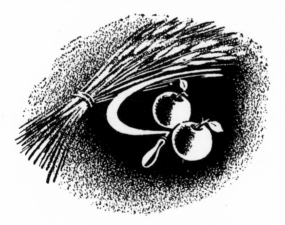

WE THANK THEE

For flowers so beautiful and sweet,
For friends and clothes and food to eat,
For precious hours, for work and play,
We thank Thee this Thanksgiving Day.

For father's care and mother's love,
For the blue sky and clouds above,
For springtime and autumn gay
We thank Thee this Thanksgiving Day!

For all Thy gifts so good and fair,
Bestowed so freely everywhere,
Give us grateful hearts we pray,
To thank Thee this Thanksgiving Day.

—*Mattie M. Renwick*

THANKSGIVING DAY

Over the river and through the wood,
  To grandfather's house we go;
    The horse knows the way
    To carry the sleigh
  Through the white and drifted snow.

Over the river and through the wood—
  Oh, how the wind does blow!
    It stings the toes
    And bites the nose,
  As over the ground we go.

Over the river and through the wood,
  Trot fast, my dapple-gray!
    Spring over the ground,
    Like a hunting-hound!
  For this is Thanksgiving Day.

Over the river and through the wood,
  And straight through the barnyard gate.
    We seem to go
    Extremely slow,—
  It is so hard to wait!

Over the river and through the wood—
  Now grandmother's cap I spy!
    Hurrah for the fun!
    Is the pudding done?
  Hurrah for the pumpkin pie!
                    —*Lydia Maria Child*

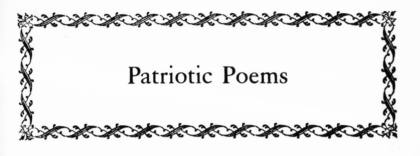

Patriotic Poems

OUR NATIVE LAND

Other countries, far and near,
Other people hold most dear;
Other countries ne'er can be
Half so dear to you and me
As our own, our native land.
By it firmly let us stand.

—*C. Phillips*

FOURTH OF JULY

Fourth of July,
　　Fourth of July,
That's when the flag
　　Goes waving by.

And the crackers crack,
　　And the popguns pop,
And the big guns boom
　　And never stop.

And we watch parades,
　　And listen to speeches,
And picnic around
　　On all the beaches.

And it usually rains,
　　And it's always hot;
But we all like Fourth
　　Of July a lot.

—Marchette Gaylord Chute

LINCOLN'S BIRTHDAY

A sacred day is this—
    A day to bless;
A day that leads to bliss
    Through bitterness.
For on this day of days,
    One wondrous morn,
In far off forest ways,
    Was Lincoln born!

Who supped the cup of tears,
    Who ate the bread
Of sorrow and of fears,
    Of war and dread;
Yet from this feast of woes,
    His people's pride,
A loved immortal rose
    All glorified!
                    —*John Kendrick Bangs*

LIKE WASHINGTON

We cannot all be Washingtons,
　　And have our birthdays celebrated;
But we can love the things he loved,
　　And we can hate the things he hated.

He loved the truth, he hated lies,
　　He minded what his mother taught him,
And every day he tried to do
　　The simple duties that it brought him.

Perhaps the reason little folks
　　Are sometimes great when they grow taller,
Is just because, like Washington,
　　They do their best when they are smaller.

　　　　　　　　　　　　　　—Unknown

MEMORIAL DAY

We plant the trees on Memorial Day,
For the soldiers who died long ago.
We plant them in the month of May
While cool winds still do blow.
                    —*Rose Florence Levy*

REMEMBERING DAY

All the soldiers marching along;
All the children singing a song;
All the flowers dewy and sweet;
All the flags hung out in the street;
Hearts that throb in a grateful way—
For this is our Remembering Day.
                    —*Mary Wright Saunders*

AN ANGEL SINGING
(*Armistice Day*)

I heard an angel singing
When the day was springing,
" Mercy, Pity, Peace
Is the world's release."

Thus he sung all day
Over the new mown hay,
Till the sun went down
And haycocks looked brown.

—William Blake

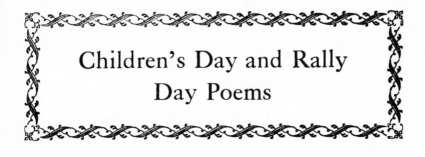

Children's Day and Rally Day Poems

GOD IS SO GOOD

God is so good that He will hear,
　　Whenever children humbly pray;
He always lends a gracious ear
　　To what the youngest child may say.

His own most holy Book declares
　　He loves good little children still;
And that He listens to their prayers,
　　Just as a tender father will.

—Jane Taylor

[157]

THE LAMB

Little lamb, who made thee?
Dost thou know who made thee?
Gave thee life, and bid thee feed
By the stream and o'er the mead;
Gave thee clothing of delight,
Softest clothing, woolly, bright;
Gave thee such a tender voice,
Making all the vales rejoice?
Little lamb, who made thee?
Dost thou know who made thee?

Little lamb, I'll tell thee;
Little lamb, I'll tell thee;
He is calléd by thy name,
For He calls Himself a Lamb.
He is meek, and He is mild,
He became a little child,
I a child, and thou a lamb

Little lamb, who made thee?
Dost thou know who made thee?

We are calléd by His name.
　Little lamb, God bless thee!
　Little lamb, God bless thee!
　　　　　—*William Blake*

I'D LAUGH TODAY

I'd laugh today, today is brief,
I would not wail for anything;
I'd use today that cannot last,
Be glad today and sing.
　　　　　—*Christina G. Rossetti*

EVERY DAY

Every day, I'm glad to say,
  I'm learning more and more:
How to be a little better
  Than I was the day before.
                          —*Elizabeth Haas*

MY WEEK

On Monday I wash my dollies' clothes,
  On Tuesday smoothly press them,
On Wednesday mend their little hose,
  On Thursday neatly dress them.

On Friday I play they're taken ill,
  On Saturday something or other,
But when Sunday comes, I say, " Lie still,
  I'm going to church with Mother."
                          —*Unknown*

THE CREATION

All things bright and beautiful,
   All creatures, great and small,
All things wise and wonderful,
   The Lord God made them all.

Each little flower that opens,
   Each little bird that sings,
He made their glowing colors,
   He made their tiny wings.

The rich man in his castle,
   The poor man at his gate,
God made them, high or lowly,
   And ordered their estate.

The purple-headed mountain,
   The river running by,
The sunset and the morning
   That brightens up the sky;

The cold wind in the winter,
  The pleasant summer sun,
The ripe fruits in the garden—
  He made them every one.

The tall trees in the greenwood,
  The meadows where we play,
The rushes by the water
  We gather every day;—

He gave us eyes to see them,
  And lips that we might tell
How great is God Almighty
  Who has made all things well.
                —*Cecil Frances Alexander*

HE PRAYETH BEST

He prayeth best, who loveth best
    All things both great and small:
For the dear God who loveth us,
    He made and loveth all.
            —Samuel Taylor Coleridge

LOVE THE BEAUTIFUL

Love the beautiful,
    Seek out the true,
Wish for the good,
    And the best do!
            —Felix Mendelssohn

DO RIGHT

Do what conscience says is right;
  Do what reason says is best;
Do with all your mind and might;
  Do your duty and be blest.

—*Unknown*

WHAT TO DO

Do all the good you can,
In all the ways you can,
In all the places you can,
At all the times you can,
To all the people you can,
As long as ever you can.

—*John Wesley*

THE HAPPY WORLD

The bee is a rover;
   The brown bee is gay;
To feed on the clover,
   He passes this way.
Brown bee, humming over,
   What is it you say?
" The world is so happy—so happy today! "
      —*William Brighty Rands*

THE STARS

What do the stars do
   Up in the sky,
Higher than the wind can blow,
   Or the clouds can fly?

Each star in its own glory
   Circles, circles still;
As it was lit to shine and set,
   And do its Maker's will.

—Christina G. Rossetti

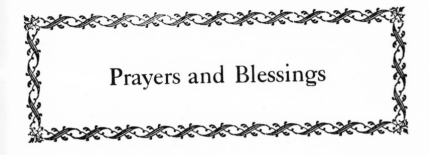

Prayers and Blessings

A THOUGHT

It is very nice to think
The world is full of meat and drink,
With little children saying grace,
In every Christian kind of place.
—Robert Louis Stevenson

TABLE BLESSINGS

O God, from whom all good gifts come,
This food, our friends, our happy home,
We ask Thy blessing. Grant we may
With grateful hearts serve Thee today.
                    —*Julia Budd Shafer*

We thank Thee, Lord, for food and drink,
    For shelter clean and warm,
And for Thy love and care for us
    That keeps us from all harm.
                    —*Bernice Ussery*

A CHILD'S PRAYER

God make my life a little light,
   Within the world to glow—
A tiny flame that burneth bright,
   Wherever I may go.

God make my life a little flower,
   That bringeth joy to all,
Content to bloom in native bower,
   Although its place be small.

God make my life a little song,
   That comforteth the sad,
That helpeth others to be strong,
   And makes the singer glad.

                —*M. Betham Edwards*

A CHILD'S GRACE

Here a little child I stand
Heaving up my either hand.
Cold as Paddocks though they be,
Here I lift them up to Thee,
For a Benizon to fall
On our meat, and on us all.

—*Robert Herrick*

TABLE BLESSING

" Father of all—God!
What we have here is of Thee;
Take our thanks and bless us,
That we may continue
To do Thy will."

—*Lew Wallace*

A CHILD'S GRACE

Some hae meat and canna eat,
    And some wad eat that want it;
But we hae meat and we can eat,
    And sae the Lord be thankit.
—Robert Burns

GENTLE JESUS, MEEK AND MILD

Gentle Jesus, meek and mild,
Look upon a little child,
Pity my simplicity,
Teach me, Lord, to come to Thee.

Fain would I to Thee be brought,
Lamb of God, forbid it not;
In the Kingdom of Thy grace
Give a little child a place.

—*Charles Wesley*

A PRAYER

Father, we thank Thee for the night
And for the pleasant morning light,
For rest and food and loving care,
And all that makes the world so fair.
Help us to do the thing we should,
To be to others kind and good,
In all we do, in all we say,
To grow more loving every day.

—Unknown

AN EVENING PRAYER

And now another day is gone,
I'll sing my maker's praise:
My comforts every hour make known,
His providence and grace.

I lay my body down to sleep,
Let angels guard my head:
And through the hours of darkness keep
Their watch around my bed.

—Reverend Isaac Watts

GOOD NIGHT

Good night! Good night!
Far flies the light;
But still God's love
Shall flame above,
Making all bright.
Good night! Good night!

—Victor Hugo

THE END

Night is come,
   Owls are out;
Beetles hum
   Round about.

Children snore
   Safe in bed,
Nothing more
   Need be said.
        —Sir Henry Newbolt

Index of Authors

[176]

Index of Authors

Index of Authors

Index of First Lines

Index of First Lines

Index of First Lines

Index of First Lines

Index of Titles

[183]

Index of Titles

Index of Titles

Index of Titles